The Marquis Cartel
James Marquis

THE
MARQUIS
CARTEL

James Marquis

CONTENTS

FORWARD

$\mathcal{F}$or those of you who did not read "1968: A Vietnam War Love Story", which is the beginning of this three-book love series, I will recap the events that led up to this, the second book in the series: "The Marquis Cartel." The name of the yacht is named after Jim's first love, who was killed in Vietnam. Tito's eternal life wish was that he and Jim would run his father's, Henry Martinez's, import/export business located in Miami, Florida. Fifteen years after the war, Jim and his new lover Ron, who he also served with in Vietnam, joined by their longtime assistant David are now employed by Henry's import/export company in Miami.

As their business grew, so did its employees. The company acquired the "TITO III," a 130' yacht to replace the Tito II, which was only 90'. Now the Tito III crew had the proper accommodations to travel the high seas of the Caribbean to focus their efforts on the expansion of their import/export operation, thus allowing them to control all ports in the Caribbean Sea.

But something was not quite right, and the deeper they dug into the company's inner workings, so did the threat of danger. Jim, Ron, and David made every effort to ensure their personal safety and that of their crew.

The Cartel had already been struck, but who ordered the hit and why? Do they stay in Miami, retreat to other ports of call, or just give up on everything?

TITO THE THIRD
March 1, 1986

The Tito III was an elegant example of a yacht built to its finest. The only way to describe the thoroughly elegant interior and exterior was, without a doubt, a floating five-star hotel. It featured four beautiful deluxe staterooms designed for maximum comfort in mind with adjoining baths, Captain's quarters, and three crew quarters that slept four each with an adjoining bath each. The whole yacht looked as if it was carved of wood and stone from the inside, giving it a French Regency styling. The dining room held twelve beautiful Queen Ann-styled African Blackwood chairs with a matching long table with fine etchings along the edges and carved artwork on the sides.

Like the Tito II, the office was located on the top deck with a 360° view. The main salon of the yacht was appointed with luxury leather-appointed furniture with metal accent pieces. Jim, Ron, and David's man cave located on the second deck just below the office was lavish. Their office was set up the same way as before. And the yacht stood ready to get underway upon command.

This time on their tour around the Caribbean, they would stop at the ports that contribute the most monthly income to the import/export business. Their first stop, Venezuela, who at last monthly report, contributed over $3 million to the firm's bottom line.

Jim shared with the team that he observed managers making a standard entrance through a door marked "storage room" in each of the offices when they arrived, and they would later reappear without explanation. He told the team that whoever was closest to that door would seal the door when they walked in. Three days later, they pulled into the Port of La Guairá in Venezuela and was guided by port authorities to a slip to tie up. They informed them that they would be docking only briefly while they found a slip to accommodate their yacht during our stay.

Accommodations were found, and that evening the Captain pulled our yacht into the slip, and Stephen, the deckhand, hooked up electricity and sewer. That evening after they were settled, Ron, Jim and David met in the man cave and discussed a strategy for tomorrow morning's arrival in their Venezuelan office. Jim led off by saying they should use more caution and be very aware of their surroundings while in the ports of calls. I think these offices are ticking time bombs, and it's our job to find the wick before it is lit. They arrived at the Venezuela office at 8:05 AM. Seeing that the manager was away from his desk, David made a direct line for the door and sealed it. The eight employees were shocked at our arrival.

The manager came out of the bathroom and immediately went to the "storage room." He noticed the seal over the handle and the lock and immediately turned in our direction. Jim took the lead by introducing himself, and Ron and David did so accordingly. They found space to get organized and proceeded with their operational checklist. This time a more in-depth review was conducted, and owners' files, if maintained, were copied and retained. The room behind the door contained a lonely computer. David was instructed to analyze and download all the information it contained. They got the password from the manager with extreme difficulty. They had to threaten him with his job before he surrendered the code.

There were several flights a day from Columbia carrying "Colombian Gold," as described in the manifest for a single client connected to a foreign company. Columbia is one of Venezuela's largest importer of corn, wheat, and other farm products. There was no mention of these imports. They spent four days in Venezuela, and as Captain John said as they pulled out of port, "Goodbye, see you next trip." Now they're off to Guatemala and Panama. Captain John picked Guatemala as our next stop, and this time they called ahead and found the yacht harbor to accommodate them for our days in port. While they were in this port, Captain John serviced the yacht (meaning fill it with petrol, food, water, ice, etc.) They went to the same procedure in this port, always looking for those interesting exceptions that they could bring to the forefront, like behind that "storage room" door was always that lonely computer.

They motored to Balboa on the Panamanian coast. It is ranked the busiest container port in Latin America. They were the only company in Panama that handled any flights or shipping of any product out or into Peru. What products are they handling, and who are they handling them for? That's our big question.

After they finished Panama, they had been at sea for almost four weeks. The Tito III operated flawlessly, and our crew maintained it immaculately at all times. The crew was top-notch. Captain John is about forty-one years old now. The ideal picture of a Captain: tall, thin, and in his white's so striking. He's been on this vessel for five years. The yacht itself is only five and a half years old, and the previous owner bought it new. Captain John leads a very casual lifestyle and has grown accustomed to indiscriminate sex in port.

This is the second yacht Chef Tommy has worked on, and he's a graduate of one of these fancy culinary colleges. He is so good-looking, about 5' 10" maybe 5'11", with dark hair, thick eyebrows, and hands like that of a surgeon. His piercing black eyes will humble you. He turns out surprising culinary delights when you least expect it.

Andrew, the chief steward, strikingly black with a dabbling of light chocolate, stands 6'3" and has short-cropped hair. With the grace of an antelope and the soft voice of a chipmunk, he provides service with care and always fulfilled with love.

Deckhand Stephen, yes, they make them stout and strong – a man that can handle the lines (ropes) of the yacht and the people at the other end who wish to be handled. His laugh was like a roar, and his chest hairs were thick to the touch. One can never resist bumping into him in a small walkway on either side of the yacht.

When the RJD LLC (Ron, Jim, and David) bought the Tito III, it was brand-new. The other yacht owner sold his yacht, and the buyer had his crew, so the seller's yacht crew were available for hire. Jim got wind of their availability and hired all of them immediately. They had worked together for five years and, by all indications, were a well-polished team. Ron drew up employment contracts, which took excellent care of them financially and ensured that their personal needs were met. Additionally, Ron had them sign nondisclosure agreements to protect everybody's privacy that boarded the Tito III.

They next headed to the Dominican Republic, finishing their tour in Jamaica and the Grand Cayman. The trip this time took almost 120 days, a month longer than the first one. When they were pulling in the harbor close to the Martinez estate, the Captain announced that something was wrong; several people were walking around the yard. When they arrived at the pier, Henry was usually there to help us with the lines, but he was missing. Captain John pulled the yacht up very close to the dock, using the yachts thrusters. Andrew and

Stephen jumped off onto the dock, and John and Timothy secured the lines to the yacht.

Immediately after docking, two policemen boarded the yacht. They had us produce all of our identification, along with ownership of the yacht. As the police were hassling them, Jim came in and asked what was going on. The police officer said there had been a double homicide at the residence, and no one was permitted to go any further. Jim told the officer that all of them work for Mr. Martinez's company, and this was our floating office. Jim asked who had been killed? The detective said the owners of this estate. It was what they all feared. And as they all turned and looked at each other, they were in complete disbelief that they just lost Herman and Mary Martinez.

After the dust settled and they were now inside the house talking with the homicide investigator. Jim asked if he was allowed to take a look at the bodies. The detective declined, stating protocol, and asked Jim if that is truly the last image of the two that he wants to see. He told them that the investigation is still ongoing, but he can tell them that they both obtained two twenty-two caliber gunshot wounds behind the ear. A small-caliber gunshot wound in this area of the head indicating an execution-style murder. Jim thought to himself, this a warning that they needed to heed. He then asked if Miami has a problem with mob violence. The detective looked keenly at Jim and said, "Yes, this was a mob hit."

After a few weeks, the homicide investigators had concluded their review. Two Hispanic males were believed to be the culprits, but a lack of evidence and a clear description led the investigation to a dead end. Whoever had done this has done it before, and they were good at it. Henry and Mary were interred in the Martinez's mausoleum alongside Tito. Jim met with the corporate attorney, who told him that Henry and Mary had left their entire estate to him.

Jim pondered on what to do with this massive estate in Miami. He was already comfortable on the yacht and did not want to be constantly reminded of the people he loved and lost, so he decided to sell the mansion. But before they could sell it, they needed to go through the house looking for any evidence that would lead them to the contact information for the actual customers of their business, for Henry surely couldn't have taken that secret to the grave with him. If so, their business would be finished before it could ever really begin. Jim, Ron, and David spread out, covering each room of the estate, leaving nothing to chance. It took them days to comb through countless records, books, filings, and loose paperwork when Jim had everyone convene with him and said they were going about this all wrong.

"If I were to hide something from the world, it wouldn't be in the most obvious place, in his records, but in either some hidden compartment or in plain enough view that you just overlook it." David agreed with Jim but said, "I think it may be in a more obvious spot for everyone assumes that rich people have secret rooms and compartments, so wouldn't that be the logical first place to look? If I were him, I'd hide it somewhere I could always see it, but no one would notice."

While searching in the large family room, Ron came across a large built-in aquarium, 6-foot-wide and 4-foot-tall. He thought it needed to be drained because no one would be there to take care of it and start to stink up the house, so he took it upon himself to drain it. While draining the aquarium, he began to collect the rocks at the bottom to throw out when he discovered a waterproof envelope. The ledger was inside, and the names and contact information of all of Henry's customers. Some of them had been customers for a multitude of years. They took the ledger and placed it under lock and key on the Tito III.

During this period, they gave the crew two weeks off with pay, telling them to prepare for an extended period at sea. They put the estate in the hands of the best realtor in town who specialized in estate sales. They set the sales price and informed him that he could fax them the details of any offers while they were out at sea. They wanted to prepare the yacht to leave port as soon as possible when everyone returned.

Ron and Jim retired to their private quarters and made passionate love for the first time in a couple of weeks. Their bodies were dripping with sweat as they feasted upon one another's flesh, embracing each other and sharing both their passions and pains. The stress of the death of the Martinez's and the following events had taken a toll on them emotionally. But that night, they were so happy to have each other that all was forgotten at that moment, and Ron dominated Jim just as Tito had many years before him.

After all the yacht preparations and stocking was complete, they met back at the yacht and immediately headed out to sea. They went to that remote island that Henry, Mary, Ron, and Jim had visited many years ago and anchored. They all agreed that they were getting too close to this ticking time bomb that was apt to explode and needed to know if and how they should get out. In all of these years, Henry trusted his client's relationships without asking any questions, and he just cashed the checks. They need to start making a survival plan, one which to be heavily detailed and inclusive of all contingencies they may experience, one far greater than the one they have now. They need to start planning immediately. Ron was put in charge of updating the survival plan, and David was to find and help patch any hole in it while Jim maintained their business dealings.

CERBERUS

*R*on started to work right away and enlisted the help of Captain John. They developed a plan that they thought addressed the critical areas of concern.

1. Armed mercenary - what type?
2. Bulletproof glass/reinforce the Tito III
3. Crew training on automatic weapons
4. Ensure pantry of shipping adequate for sixty days at sea
5. Purchase all of the state-of-the-art electronic systems necessary
6. Satellite phones
7. The rank of seniority on the yacht during an attack

After reviewing the security list and determining that they were not in the security business and needed a professional, Ron contacted GYS Security Solutions's international office, which had an office in Miami. One of their account officers made an appointment to visit the yacht. Ron, Jim, and David met with Mr. Davenport in the man cave on the TITO III the following day and went into great detail about their concerns about the Cartel hit at the Hernandez estate.

They explained this was a large import/ export business in the Caribbean, and they have begun investigating their shippers and vendors in greater detail than in the past. They want to make sure that while they are in their floating office, and no matter what port docked at, that they would have taken every precaution to safeguard all onboard.

Mr. Davenport recommended that they consider a retired Navy Seal with both nautical and land combat experience. He said he had the ideal candidate in mind and that he will make him available immediately. He said he would like to arrange a meeting as soon as possible. Two days later, at nine in the morning, a gigantic black man requested to board the TITO III. His name was Simon: thirty-four years old, 6'4", and probably weighed about 250 lbs. Polite, as polite could be, he inquired as to our names and the crew's names, and just like that, he memorized everybody and ranked them in executive value.

Simon said he was briefed by Mr. Davenport about their concerns and felt that he could accomplish whatever they wanted with their proper support. His fee was two hundred fifty thousand dollars a year, which he itemized accordingly. It was all more than reasonable with the expertise and security Simon was providing. If anything, Jim thought he was getting one hell of a deal for the price of complete peace of mind.

They spoke for a while, asking questions back and forth. Simon's knowledge of nautical dangers that they may face and how to counteract them was more than impressive. They ask Captain John to take him on a tour of the yacht and show him the extra deluxe bedroom, which would be his private quarters. They then agreed to his fee and asked him to start immediately. Just having him onboard provided a feeling of tranquility that they so desperately needed. They all felt safe again.

Outfitting the Yacht

Simon formed a laundry list for purchases for the yacht that seemed almost endless. They never knew the sheer volume of electronic equipment made to either spy on/locate people or alert a person of pending danger. Automatic weapons, ammunition, and all types of explosives were loaded at various ports in the Caribbean. Through GYS, Simon had access to almost all military equipment that is manufactured anywhere in the world. After they finished loading the equipment safely and lightly retrofitting the yacht, they set out for the Grand Caymans. They pulled into the Yacht Club and Marina in the Caymans and decided to anchor there for a few days, and soon after, they would finish up by stopping in a few ports in the Caribbean. While they were there, Simon made arrangements for a complete refitting of the yacht with bulletproof windows, additional electronic systems and reinforcing the yacht's bow.

While the yacht was in dry dock, they stayed at the Rum Point hotel. They booked two deluxe suites and had plenty of room for six people. Both had an Oceanview with a private entrance and over 2000 ft.^{2} They were in the Grand Caymans for over two weeks, and our legs were getting anxious for the sea. They booked Simon into a suite between Jim, Ron, and David and the crew.

When they boarded the TITO III after the refitting was completed, everyone felt as if they were finally home. They looked around, and everything looked the same; they didn't notice anything that had changed. However,

Simon instantly looked at the bulletproof windows' thickened glass plating and checked out the improved communications deck. Captain John said, "Are you ready to sail?" Stephen and Andrew tended to the lines, and the dock hands untied them and threw them aboard. They were off to an undetermined location.

While in the Grand Caymans, Ron set up seven bank accounts, one for each crew member, including the office staff. The crew's payroll would be deposited in their Grand Caymans' bank accounts. The import/export business's monthly profit would be divided by three and deposited in the appropriate Grand Cayman account. Ron then took the responsibility of depositing the excess funds of Jim, David, and himself to various banks around the world. Ron took the time to fly to Europe and set up bank accounts in Switzerland for twelve different corporations managed through four different LLCs filed in Miami. Ron would keep moving funds to various banks, always keeping the balances equal in fairness to the company's three owners.

Simon instructed Captain John to sail out into open waters to test the radar system that identifies incoming boats of various sizes within a 100-mile radius. He suggested they stay at sea for a couple of days to ensure that they're not being followed by any vessel so they would be able to dock at a port of our choice. While they were at sea, Simon went over all of the added security measures added to the Tito III while in dry dock. They were all greatly impressed that bulletproof glass was installed in every window, and the yacht itself was reinforced without adding too much weight.

The ship's hall had been enhanced with a bulletproof material that was light in weight and did not diminish the vessel's speed. They were entirely impressed with all of the electronics. Some cameras would visually patrol 360 degrees under the surface of the yacht and had night vision. The boat was also supplemented with cameras that patrolled in a 360° radius around the yacht's exterior. If there were an advancing boat, the cameras would set off an alert that could be heard all through the yacht. Simon informed them that this was his call to action when this alert sounded; just follow his instructions.

While at sea Jim, Ron, and David met and decided to purchase a yacht club at each of the Caribbean islands. This would provide them a way of laundering funds and having an on-call port of call to escape to. The yacht clubs they purchase must have at least a 130-foot-long tie-up for their vessel, gas facilities, stores/markets, and proximity to banking facilities. David was charged with the responsibility to identify potential yacht clubs on each of the islands. He would call ahead and make appointments with the potential sellers so Ron could meet with them. Due to the secrecy behind their transactions, Ron was the only one that met with the potential sellers.

While Ron and David were busy locating and buying yacht clubs around the Caribbean, Jim investigated the ledger found in the aquarium in Henry's house. It contained a list of six names:

1. Carlos Lehder – Colombia's most feared drug baron
2. Gerson Galvez – Peru's (aka "Snail" he was called the new El Chapo)
3. Joaquin "El Chapo" Guzman – Columbia and México - Panama
4. Erick "El Pocho" Salvador – Guatemala
5. Christopher "Dudus" Michael Coke – Jamaica
6. Santiago Luis Polanco – Dominican Republic

After reviewing the ledger in detail, including the profits made from each of the kingpins, Jim shut the book, laid it on his desk, and said to himself: "What did they get ourselves into"?

That night over dinner, there was a lot to discuss, from the drug kingpins who were their major clients to the yacht harbors in the major ports of call identified by David as potential marinas to purchase. Jim started off the discussion. He informed everyone, including Simon, that the people they do business with are known killers and have a large syndicate surrounding them. Simon's expertise will be necessary to safeguard our vessel and all of us from potential attacks. David identified six yacht clubs that Jim and Ron could investigate for purchase.

Simon was the first to phone his head office to inquire if they or any of their sister companies had provided protection to any of the Marquis's known clientele, running down the list of names. His office replied yes, all of them! He then requested briefing papers on all the special instructions included in the protection plans to be faxed to the ship as soon as possible.

Jim had a different plan entirely. He wanted to get inside one of the most dangerous Jamaican organizations and hopefully enlist their support in carrying out the illegal part of their operation.

David provided Jim and Ron with a list of yacht harbors to consider purchasing.

1. Montego Bay Yacht Club – Jamaica
2. Royal Jamaica Yacht Club – Jamaica
3. The Marina Casa de Campo – Dominican Republic (Slips up to 270')
4. Marina CC – Dominican Republic (slips up to 150')
5. Grand Cayman Yacht Club – Grand Cayman, Islands
6. Georgetown Yacht Club – Grand Caymans

Club de Yates de Balboa – Panama (Panama YC would cover Latin American ports.)

Ron had his work cut out for him. How do you figure a fair market price for a yacht club that you're willing to pay any amount for? Money was no object in these purchases. They need them for a quick getaway to another port of call at any given time, day or night.

As in any major purchase, they discussed them over dinner and told chef Tommy to make a rather expensive one to commemorate this monumental event. It turned out to be lamb shank over rice with broccoli and homemade bread pudding topped with whipped cream for dessert. It was just the meal to celebrate our new ventures.

Ron and Jim retired to the private quarters and ended the night in internal bliss where they slept until nine the next morning. Since both of them woke up with morning wood, another hour had to be added before the two would truly get out of bed to eat breakfast.

The team set down and rated the importance of each yacht harbor to our operation; the following represents a list of ports in order of importance:

1. Venezuela
2. Panama-Guatemala
3. Jamaica-Dominican Republic
4. Grand Caymans

Purchasing four locations in the Caribbean would give them the right opportunity to evade most people following or trying to find their exact location.

Ron spent most of his time devoted to purchasing a new yacht club, while Jim was pursuing the King of the largest cutthroat gang in Jamaica.

THE ACQUISITION

*R*on was designated the representative of the RJD Import/Export to purchase the yacht clubs. Of course, all details of the purchase were always discussed over dinner. They decided that the first club that Ron would pursue would be at the port of Panama City, the Balboa Yacht Club. It was a well-known club with a view of the Panama Canal. They decided to dock the yacht at the Royal Jamaica yacht club while they were negotiating the purchase of the Panamanian club. On Monday, Ron flew into Panama City and checked into the Hilton Garden Inn.

That night he visited the Balboa club for the first time. The restaurant was loaded with customers, and as he checked in with the harbormaster at the club, he was told that he just made it in for nearly all of the slips were occupied except for only three 150' foot slips. Ron was duly impressed with the club as it also had a view of the Panama Canal. Further investigation revealed that it was the oldest and most well-known club in Panama.

The next day he made it a point to go to the club and meet the owner. To his surprise, the owner was not on the property. The highest-ranking person there was the yacht club manager by the name of José. Ron asked how he could get in touch with the owner of the club. José gave Ron his phone number and told him his name was Freddie. He also suggested not to call him before noon.

Ron also asked as to where the owner lived. José replied that he has never met the owner and he didn't know where he lives. The owner's instructions were always transmitted by email, letter, phone call, or by the owner's friend, Devon. Ron found this arrangement quite peculiar. He called Jim on the yacht and informed him that he was flying back and that he would negotiate the sale of the Panama club over the phone.

When Ron got back to the yacht, he reviewed all of his notes on the club and placed a call to Freddie at 2 p.m. Freddie answered the phone, and Ron introduced himself as the owner of RJD LLC. Without skipping a beat, he told Freddie that he was interested in purchasing his yacht club. Freddie immediately said, "It's not for sale." Ron said, "Name a ridiculous price, and I will buy it." At the other end of the phone, Ron could hear Freddie laughing, and then he said to Devon, "There's some asshole on the phone that wants to buy the yacht club and said, name your price." Ron could hear Devon in the background saying $20 million; Freddie laughed and said, "Nobody's got that much money to spend on our yacht club. It would take years to make your return on your investment."

Ron spoke up and said, "It's a deal. I'll take it!" Ron asked Freddie where he would like the money wired to, and Ron would draw up the necessary paperwork for his signature. He then inquired where Freddie's attorney would like the documents faxed? Ron continued by saying that all the negotiations to transfer this property could be handled through an attorney of Freddie's choice in Panama.

Freddie, floored with Ron's response, gave Ron his attorney's number, and negotiations were thus underway. In three days, they finalized the purchase and transferred everything over. When Freddie got off the phone with his attorney, he cautioned Ron, "They're going to be after all of you. There's no place that you can hide. You're marked for death".

Freddie instantly hung up the phone. Ron was blindsided by Freddie's ominous remark. He did not fully understand the criminality behind their apparently legal business. He let Jim handle the questionable affairs of their business. Ron only dealt with the legal portion of all their ventures, while Jim managed everything else. They have been forewarned. Henry and Mary's death by execution was no random event, and now this warning tonight. Ron felt something strange brewing in the air, but time would only tell if he is right. Jim told Ron to hold off on any purchases in Venezuela until we can have a full security detail escort you and ensure your safety. It seemed South America would be more troublesome than previously planned. But in the meantime, they are now the proud owners of a yacht club in Panama, Ron's first lone purchase, and their money couldn't have made it any easier.

Ron's next location was Jamaica. David had identified two yacht clubs to purchase; both of them had slips that exceeded 130'. Ron flew into Jamaica and immediately did his due diligence on both clubs and found them in excellent condition and prime locations with restaurants, grocery, fuel, and yacht maintenance facilities. Like he did in Panama, he threw money at it and purchased both yacht clubs for $35M.

Last but not least were the yacht clubs in the Caymans. They decided to head for the Grand Caymans and stay at the Georgetown yacht club. When Ron flew back to Jamaica, he flew back with two more yacht clubs. Ron was becoming a natural at the real estate game, and with each purchase, he managed to negotiate an even lower purchasing price than the deal he had struck before.

When Ron returned to the yacht, Simon immediately met with him informing him that he had talked to GYS and had arranged additional security detain to join them in Venezuela. Ron was ecstatic, for he could finally close all of the deals he had previously planned. He thought he might have had to wait a while till they could close a deal in Venezuela, jeopardizing their entire operation.

Ron asked Simon, "When can we leave?"

Simon replied, "Jim already booked us tickets for tomorrow."

Ron thought how much he loved Jim. He did not have to say a word, and Jim had already taken care of things for him. He is such a great partner.

The next morning Ron and Simon were on the next flight out to Maracaibo, Venezuela. Ron asked Simon if he could be referred to as Mr. Marquis during the trip due to the previous threat in Panama. He was afraid that using his first name could possibly cause them to be attacked. Simon said he would phone GYS and tell them to only refer to you as Mr. Marquis.

As soon as they landed, a 4-man security detail greeted them. "Hello, my name is Raphaël. I'm the lead agent of this unit," said this short but stocky Hispanic man. My men are Victor, Kody, and Miguel. We will be escorting you on your travels today, Mr. Marquis.

"It's a pleasure to meet you all, and I hope that this will be an incredibly boring and uneventful job for you, Ron said with a chuckle. Raphaël laughed as well and said, we wish the same as well, Mr. Marquis.

Ron and Simon then were escorted to an all-black SUV with tinted windows, where they now departed in the harbor's direction. Raphaël continued, "The itinerary states that you wish to check out two prospective yachting clubs, correct? We took the liberty of scouting them out before your arrival and gathering information on the owners, their contact information, affiliates, and who manages their properties with rough figures on how much the property is currently valued. Ron was astounded. "You don't miss a beat, do you, Raphaël?" Raphaël replied, "No, sir, it's my job not to miss anything at all."

Before they arrived at the first yacht club, Ron called the manager and asked if the owner was in. The manager told him that he should be returning any time about now and he could take a message. Ron said, "No need, we will be arriving at the club in thirty minutes and will meet with your boss directly."

Ron hung up immediately; Raphaël laughed and said, "You are very direct when you do business, sir." While staring out the window, Ron replied, "I learned in this trade you have to be."

When they arrived, they got out of the SUV, walked directly to the manager's office, and asked if the owner had arrived. The manager escorted them to the back, where the owner was sitting by the water smoking a cigar. "Good evening Mr. Santiago, my name is Mr. Marquis, and I am here to make an offer on this establishment," Ron said as he shook his hand and took a seat next to him while resting his right leg on his left knee. "Not for sale, now get off my property," Mr. Santiago remarked.

Ron continued, "Now I heard that one before, but what if I am willing to make you an offer so ridiculous that you have no other option but to say yes?" Mr. Santiago sat up in his chair and took a deep puff of his cigar.

"This is not your average sailing club; this club has a pedigree of racing. It's a tradition that we have kept for many years and do not intend to stop now, Mr. Marquis."

Ron interjected, "I am in no way, shape or form trying to end any lasting traditions here, Mr. Santiago. I am only interested in keeping a footing in Venezuela, and your club meets all our expectations. You can keep all your traditions and the money you make by placing bets on "boats" every weekend."

Mr. Santiago looked at Ron with surprise. "So, what are you offering, Marquis?"

Ron leaned forward, "I am offering you $18 million US. We know your club is currently worth around $12 million, including what you take in from all club activities annually without subtracting expenses. My offer is more than fair, Santiago. I offer 1.5 times your total annual revenue plus all your assets, including the property. Why? Because I want this deal inked out today. I'm a very busy man Santiago. Ron then pulled out the paperwork and slid it in front of him.

"Bella, get me a pen," Mr. Santiago yelled. Ron looked at him and asked, "Aren't you going to meet with your lawyer first?"

Mr. Santiago then replied, "No, I never trusted those devils. I handle all paperwork myself, like my father and his father before him. We are men, not cowards. I see how you talk and carry yourself, and I don't see any coward in you. So, let's make a fucking deal."

They both made a few adjustments to the contract keeping the yacht races, and they completed the deal that evening. Simon told Ron that they should carry out the next meeting tomorrow and he should retire to the hotel and get some rest.

When leaving, they noticed a car that seemed to be following them as they left the yacht club. Raphaël ordered Victor to make the next right and pull over as he and two of his members exited the vehicle with SMGs tucked in their blazers. A brown sedan with four men inside slowly passed by their SUV, staring at the security detail, and then turned at the next corner. "Let's roll!" Yelled Raphaël as he slapped the top of the SUV three times and got in. They sped towards the hotel and dropping Ron off with the entire security detail in tow sans Victor, for he went to park the SUV in a non-conspicuous location so that nobody would recognize the SUV; he also changed the plates.

While in the room, Simon and Raphaël began to talk about what just transpired. "I guess your trip isn't as boring as we hoped, Mr. Marquis, but don't you worry, you are completely safe with us, for we are the best," Raphaël said with a big reassuring smile on his face. "We got their license plate number, but we doubt that would be of any use to us; cartels constantly recycle little beaters like that. They use them once for a hit job and either chop them up for parts or switch them up and respray them to go again. We should be more cautious when we go out tomorrow."

Ron asked, "Do you think Santiago is directly connected to those men? Simon replied, "If not directly, indirectly. It's hard to make a large deal like the one you made here without somebody finding out that you."

The next day Ron called the next yacht club owner directly and scheduled to meet at a local seafood restaurant that he owned by the marina for lunch. The restaurant was closed especially for them, and they made their way to the back to meet Mr. Klein. Mr. Klein was an Argentinian-born German with long brunette locks and villainously handsome. He was relatively young to be an owner of a yacht club, which means he either came from wealth or that his business savvy is second to none.

Sitting next to him was his lawyer and what seemed to be his girlfriend, who had a jaded look upon her face. She looked as if she could have been a movie star and acted just as bratty as she chewed her gum and played with her hair. "Mr. Marquis, my lawyer has looked over the paperwork that you so kindly faxed us before our meeting, and everything is in order. My only question is, why would you want to disturb this delicate little ecosystem of ours?"

Ron replied, " I don't know what you mean." Klein continued, "Well, you will. But enough with the small talk, let's get down to business. Your offer of $18.2 Million is more than fair so let's dot the I's and finish things up." As soon as they signed the contract, Klein thanked Ron and left the table. As Ron made his way outside, he heard tires screech and Simon pulling him to the floor, saying, "Get down!" Gunfire erupted out of the same brown sedan they saw yesterday, striking Kody multiple times and hitting Raphaël as they traded rounds. Simon managed to shoot the driver in the head, killing him instantly and sending the car barreling into a wall. The other three men got out and continued to open fire but were quickly put down.

"Kody's not going to make it, boss," whispered Victor.

"He did his job and kept the client safe; we will get him the help he needs when we get the client to safety," Simon replied. They loaded Kody into the back of the car and took off. While driving, Simon requested a medivac chopper and reported the incident to GYS.

"The chopper will be ready to go to the airport in fifteen minutes; let's try to do everything we can to patch you two up before we get there," Simon said. Ron thanked everyone for saving his life. As they exited the SUV, Simon told him that the company had chartered him a private flight to immediately get him back home while GYS further investigates this incident.

While on the jet, Ron talked to Simon and asked him if this could be their little secret. He didn't want Jim to find out because he already lost one love of his life.

"I don't want him afraid that this will happen again to him. I want us to be happy, not fearing for our lives." Simon agreed under one condition. That he doesn't go back there, and they must enlist more help to get that area into proper control. Ron agreed, as well.

They had finally completed their plan and now owned seven yacht clubs in the Caribbean where they can escape to at any given time, night and day. There would always be guaranteed dockside tie-downs for their yacht at all their clubs upon their arrival. Now they could start funneling millions of dollars through these locations as their bank accounts were overflowing with money even though they just spent a little north of $112 million purchasing yacht clubs.

The next morning Ron, Jim and David had a meeting with Simon. They explained their upcoming plans about controlling the import-export business in the Caribbean and beyond. They had already told Simon that they had just bought seven yacht clubs, and that protection was now even more critical. Ron reminded them that all of them had been tagged for death.

"It feels like a cartel war is coming," David said with a shudder.

Simon followed with, "It may be that you are now setting yourselves up to be the next cartel, the *Marquis Cartel*." Jim's suggested to Simon that he should consider adding staff because the Tito III is 130' long, and that's a lot of deck space to cover for one mercenary. Simon agreed that another helping hand with his level of skills would be an asset. He stated that he has an ideal candidate, Adam, who he had worked with quite a bit, and would like to invite him to the ship for an interview.

Jim spoke up immediately and said, "I'll fly him to the Grand Caymans at his earliest convenience, no appointment necessary. Just tell him we are parked at the Georgetown Yacht Club. But the only issue that we need to address is that we currently don't have any additional accommodations. All of our estate rooms are currently occupied, leaving only one smaller crew room." Simon spoke up and said that was no problem; he can bunk in with him. They had shared living quarters before on many assignments like this and with far less luxurious accommodations. Jim said, "If you're comfortable with those living arrangements, so am I; go ahead and give Adam a call."

Two days later, Adam was dockside requesting permission to board the Tito III. Ron, Jim, David, and Simon all joined Adam in the man cave for a round of drinks and relaxed conversation. Jim took the liberty of introducing Ron and David while they took a moment just to admire Simon's friend. "Adam's quite impressive," Ron whispered. He was just as tall as Simon with a bodybuilder's physique. His long blonde hair flowed about twelve inches past his shoulders. Gaze a bit lower, and Adam appeared even to put horses to shame. The bulge in his tight white pants was so large everyone first assumed it must have been a weapon. Adam had a nicely tanned white body, and his skin looked as smooth as silk.

Simon explained the emergency procedures already in place for the yacht in the event of an attack by either amphibious assault, terrestrial, or the rare occasion a helicopter, missile, etc., might attack them. He said that an additional staff member is needed because the length of the yacht was 130'. That would require two exceptionally trained mercenaries to cover that much footage defensively under any attack.

Adam questioned if they had any attacks on the yacht. Simon's reply was negative, but they have received threats that they are taking seriously. He went on to say, "Ron, Jim, and David are exceptionally wealthy individuals who control an import/export empire in the Caribbean. If we retain your services, Adam, our responsibility to them is to take the bullet first."

"Everything we do must protect them from any danger, large or small. From now on, we have to screen all unknown individuals outside our sphere of influence," Simon continued, "The nine of us onboard the Tito III can now be considered family. As of this moment, no one is allowed within our family without scrutiny."

Ron, Jim, and David asked Adam a round of questions and found him to be very gentle but extremely masculine at the same time. He had served with Simon on eight different assignments over the last six years. They have a very close relationship, and it would be a pleasure to provide his services to the RJD, LLC owners. With Simon's outstanding recommendation, Adam was hired at Simon's same salary and was asked to start immediately. When he arrived in the Grand Caymans, his backpack and duffel bag contained all of his worldly possessions.

That night was the first time that Simon and Adam have been able to spend any time together since their last assignment three months ago. Both of them have missed each other's arms and the special moments they used to spend together. When Adam finally got his clothes off, his body was gently bronzed all over, and his uncut manhood was an impressive six-inch flaccid hog surrounded by loads of golden pubic hair. His massive balls hung down with authority as he began to pant like a bull in heat.

Simon could never resist Adam. Once he had Adam in his arms, that's all it took for him to completely surrender to his power and be dominated so gracefully that the enduring pain was only pleasure. Simon would caress Adam's entire body before they both came to a climax. They so cherished their time together and wished their assignments would never end. During their off periods, they have previously discussed living together between assignments. But GYS forbids relationships amongst team members. Emotions on the battlefield could get you or your client killed.

The next day, Simon and Adam secretly went over the entire crew list and had GYS perform a complete background investigation on each crew member. Simon knew of Captain John only by their brief sexual encounters but never thoroughly investigated his past. Both Simon and Adam knew they had to remove their personal lives' closeness to conform to their employer's rules. GYS Secure Solutions provided all of the background information on the crew of the Tito III. The only blurb that came up was on Stephen, the deckhand. His file indicated that he had been arrested three times for petty robbery. Each time he was arrested, he was thrown out of court because of insufficient evidence or the accuser not wanting to press charges.

Simon summoned Stephen to the man cave. He inquired as to his three petty robberies recorded in his background information. Simon said he wanted a detailed explanation of each event. Stephen was surprised that this information surfaced. He asked why they were asking him this now after being on board for over a year. Simon pointed out that he was here to answers his questions, not the other way around.

Simon insisted that Stephen go into great detail about each robbery.

Stephen went on to explain each event, "When I was eighteen years old, I took a leather jacket from a store. The security guard chased me, but I got away. When I got home, my mother saw the jacket and asked where I got it, knowing that I didn't have the money to buy it. She kept at me until I told her that I took it. She instructed him to take it back to the store immediately. When I took it back to the store, they called the police and reported the theft."

"The next one came about eight months after the coat episode; I was buying groceries at the market. On my way to check-out, I took four magazines off the rack next to the checkout counter and put them under my coat. I was caught doing that and reported to the police."

"The last time was on my nineteenth birthday. I was celebrating with friends, and we all went to the liquor store to get some beer. Three of them went into the store, and two of them distracted the clerk while I walked out with two six-packs of beer. The store owner called the cops on us, but I was the only one taken into custody because I took the beer."

"That is the total account of my criminal past. Since then, I have been a good little boy, and the only illegal activity I have performed is in bed with another man. I am sure you can understand that crime. All of the crew are happy to have you onboard Adam to secure our safety and the safety of Ron, Jim, and David. I'm sure that the entire crew will cooperate in any way to support your security."

Simon was satisfied with Steven's account of his criminal record, but he felt uneasy about him personally. There was a tenseness in his body language that communicated secrecy and avoidance. He told Adam to keep a close eye on him from now on.

THE GRAND MARQUIS

$\mathcal{J}$im and Ron have been together for over seven years now. They are such a well-suited couple that one cannot tell where one of them starts and the other ends. They're like a force of nature, blended into one beautiful specimen of manliness that is simply unmatched in the world around us. They possess the personality, stunning looks (as many gay men do), and they communicate with such eloquence that they could sway the hearts of both the common man and one of royalty. They are simply unchallenged in either arena. They are sexually so attracted to each other that another man can never truly catch their eyes. And each time they make love, it's like a brand-new adventure they embark on. Each time they surprise each other with the level of their sexual satisfaction. When the love for your partner is so assured, your climaxes erupt like a geyser. Tonight, they made love in celebration of Ron's victories in the Caribbean.

One of the major areas that they did not consider in their overall plan was how to manage the yacht clubs with strict discipline. They needed to ensure the managers would turn a blind eye to the money funneling through the company accounts. Of course, David would be handling all the record-keeping and bank deposits via wire transfer, but actual deposits had to be made in the banking locations through the yacht clubs. That's where they needed one of their men in charge.

Jim, Ron, and David asked the crew to join them in a meeting on the back deck. There was a self-service bar, and Jim said, "Help yourselves to anything you wanted to drink because we're going to have a long talk and need your help." Then they told them that they had purchased seven yacht clubs in the Caribbean. The crew was totally surprised. Ron asked if they knew of anybody looking for a management position who would be 100% loyal to us. Captain John mentioned the guy that he brought to the New Year's party. "He's an experienced manager as well as a boat captain, and he is currently looking for a new job." Ron asked Captain John for his friend's contact information and let him know that he would be reaching out to him this afternoon.

Next to speak was deckhand Stephen. "I know a guy named Wayne, who is looking for a job. He's kind of on the rough side, but I know he would be loyal. He's the type of guy that would be loyal to whoever paid him the highest." Again, Ron asked for his information and told Stephen to get in touch with him.

Timothy and Andrew both spoke up and gave their referrals, which Ron noted for both, and assured Timothy and Andrew that he would contact them this afternoon.

In one short meeting, Ron received four referrals for managers that he could use. Since Ron had purchased seven yacht clubs in four countries, he could use a loyal manager for each of the four countries. Ron interviewed all of the individuals by telephone and told them to standby for a money order for enough money to fly to the Grand Caymans.

Within two days, all four of them were on board. Captain John's ex-lover, Alex, was bilingual, two inches shorter than Captain John, with black hair and a small mustache. Chef Tim recommended Butch, and he was that in his appearance. He stood about 5' 10", medium build, and talked with a southern accent. He wasn't bilingual; however, he did know enough Spanish to get by. Steward Andrew referred Jamison. Ron remembered him from the New Year's Eve Party; how could one forget him. A strikingly handsome black man, 6' 3", slender, with size 14 shoes. One can only imagine what other areas on the man were large. He was bilingual and came from one of the small French Polynesian islands.

Deckhand Stephen introduced Wayne to Ron with a big smile on his face. Ron immediately asked, "What's with the smile?" Stephen said, "Wayne's 100% gay, I bet you couldn't tell." Ron was surprised because he didn't pick up any gay vibe from this butch appearing guy. He was as average as average gets in all areas but very handsome. Ron asked him about him coming off as a straight man. He said he did so mainly for the thrill; it was really fun to pick up unsuspecting straight guys and try to turn them. Even though Wayne didn't speak a lick of Spanish, he had a big old smile that could be interpreted in any language.

While the prospective managers were on board, Simon ran a background check on all of them. Areas of concern showed up on all four of them. Simon sorted out all the information and met with the ones of concern before they left for their duty stations. Three of the four had old information on file.

Wayne, the butch appearing manager, had recently been arrested in Miami for kidnapping and holding a businessman for ransom, and he's currently on probation. Simon called GYS to get detailed information on his probation and conviction. It took almost two days, and the fax came in outlining both events. The authorities were able to arrest him and rescued the hostage without harm. The hostage did not press charges for some reason, but he did stand trial and was convicted of kidnapping and given one-year probation with the restriction that he could not leave Miami. Now they had a problem on their hands.

Simon once again called GYS and had them inquire about his probation status and if he had received permission to leave Miami for any reason. They got right back to him, stating that he had not received permission to leave Miami and he is now in violation of his probation.

Simon and Adam both asked Wayne to meet with them in the man cave. Upon his arrival, he looked perplexed and knew something was up. Simon started, "We know that you are on parole and that you've violated it by being here." Somewhat shaken, Wayne asked, "Is there any way that you could arrange for me to get permission to work outside of Miami."

Adam said, "You're asking a lot from people you don't even know. And people who don't trust you because you lied to them."

Wayne began explaining that the hostage situation wasn't how it seemed and had been part of a role-playing game with a rich, gay client. "The client wanted to role-play a hostage situation, and it quickly went south. When they acted out the sexual abuse and failed escape scene, he accidentally made a real 911 call on what was supposed to be a fake phone. I hung up, not knowing if the police would show up to the call since it sounded so fake and obviously sexual."

"But the cops did come, and when they questioned the rich jerk about the incident, he wouldn't say a word to defend me because he didn't want his name in the paper. So they arrested me. He was wealthy enough to buy off the police but didn't do a thing for my conviction and probation. I've learned my lesson dealing with faggots."

Simon told him to leave, and he would get back to him later that day. After he left, Simon called his office and had them make arrangements with the probation officer to permit him to work outside of Miami for the company. They pulled a few strings, and as long as the Marquis employed him, he would be fulfilling his probation requirements and allowed to work abroad. Wayne was now indebted to the company and had to prove that they made the right decision by taking a chance on him.

After they understood all the background issues, Ron, Jim, and David decided to hire all four men to be their new managers of the yacht clubs they just purchased. Since the Tito III has an extra crew room with four bunks, they would stay on board for a week of cross-training and indoctrination into the import-export business before starting their particular club assignments. They had not yet decided as to which club each would manage.

For the next five days, all seven of them spent breakfast, lunch and dinner together, reviewing most of the records obtained from previous operational reviews. On the sixth day, Ron turned on the television in the man cave to identify the top producing ports. Now it was up to them to make a recommendation for their assignments. GYS has the power to make all of the things happen. They're very well-known and respected and have their hands in almost every country worldwide.

Wayne spoke up, "I'd like to be assigned to the Grand Caymans. They speak English, and the men are exceptionally good looking."

Jamison spoke next, "How about Venezuela for me? It looks like a very challenging assignment, and I'm fluent in Spanish. And if you can't tell, I kind of have that international look due to my blended heritage. So, I won't stand out in the crowd."

Alex said, "I'll take Panama if that's okay. I like the idea of watching those boats go down the Canal while I work. And I see that I will be handling a few offices in Central America as well, which I'm sure will be a challenging job. No worries, I'm up to it.'

Last but not least was Butch. He simply replied, "Well, looks like I'm going to Jamaica then. Perfectly fine with me; I have always been rather fond of those pretty Jamaican asses. Most everybody in Jamaica speaks English as their primary language, so my little Spanglish will work fine.

One night over dinner, Ron, Jim, and David started to strategize the Caribbean operation. They had fifteen ships operating out of the Caribbean to ports along the United States' eastern coast and many ports in Europe. They had ten planes operating in South America between Peru to Colombia and two ports in Venezuela, Panama, Guatemala, and Honduras. They started identifying their competition. Their largest competition was a company with four ships that primarily sailed the East Coast of the United States and Portugal.

Ron suggested that they put a plan together to buy out their competitors and consolidate their operation. They would have to generate even more money than they currently have by selling off some assets and taking on some debt to make this plan more than just a pipe dream, but they could do it. If they could pull this off, they would then control all of the Caribbean exports whatever they may go.

David asked, "What will you do if they don't want to sell? Jim spoke up, "I'll take care of that." So, they planted the seed for a whole new organization to be born outside of the import/export business.

It took a lot of Ron's legal research to uncover the three companies' owners that were their competitors. Ron took the contact information down and took it home to give to Jim. Between them, they were discussing tactics on how to best approach these individual owners. Again, they had no idea how to price the business. It would just be money that talks. Ron and Jim decided that Ron would contact them and establish an appointment and present them with an open offer to buy the company. The paperwork gave them forty-eight hours to accept or decline the offer.

Jim's approach was quite simple. If they resist, beat the shit out of them until they sign the paperwork. During the last few months, Jim traveled with a circle that he had not traveled with before. He has always been fascinated by the rougher individuals; they seem to stimulate his sexual fantasies. He had gotten in with the inner sanctum of one of the roughest cutthroat gangs in Jamaica and various ports in the Caribbean. He hooked up with "King" for a couple of weeks, and that was a wild ride.

Jim had to admit to Ron that he did end up cheating on him. "I hate to talk about it, but it was not love I enjoyed outside of our relationship; it was purely sexual fantasy and business. Being able to climb to the top of one of the roughest criminal organizations' inner sanctum is an outstanding achievement. I think they will help us if I asked for their assistance. Ron understood Jim's goal in pursuing the Jamaican organization and was glad that Jim could use them to help if need be. While Ron was busy traveling in the Caribbean buying businesses, Jim made contact with the King of the Jamaican gang.

KING'S CROWN

*E*verybody called him King. Jim was no different. Jim gave him a call and asked how he was, and if he missed him? King, laughing over the phone, said, "Sure, Jimmy, who wouldn't miss that sweet sausage of yours."

Jim said, "Do you want to get together again?

King said, "Ya, how about today at five – my place, you know where it is."

Jim replied, "Affirmative."

It was about 4:45 when Jim was walking up the steps of King's elaborate townhouse. One of King's many bodyguards answered the door and said, "You're a little bit early for your appointment, aren't you? Jim walked in without answering. He wasn't going to be high-handed by some lowly bodyguard when he is going to fuck the King. Jim sat in a plush chair in the living room while a servant approached him and asked if he wanted a drink. Jim replied, "Scotch and soda tall with lime."

Just then, King walked in clad in his silk bathrobe and polo slippers with the biggest grin you could ever see on a handsome Jamaican man. He sat down next to Jim and gave him a kiss, which Jim immediately returned. The conversation started with the amount of time it had been since they'd both seen each other. Three weeks, they agreed, was far too long. Jim's drink arrived, and so did one for King. As they sipped on their cocktails, King disrobed Jim down to his birthday suit. Now all Jim had to do was open King's silk robe.

They decided to set the drinks down and headed to the bedroom. King was only 5'9" and 160 pounds. When he was with Jim, he was not at all threatening. It was like flipping a switch that turned off the head of the criminal organization and turned on the most passive, beautiful black man there has ever been in this world. He had a shaved head shined with some oil, displayed a six-pack, and had 8" inches swinging between his legs. Jim was amazed that this seemingly very gentle and non-threatening person was the leader of Jamaica's most notorious criminal organization.

King gave great head; he loved to smother Jim's body with kisses and work his black magic on every part of him.

Jim took pleasure in King's ability to be so passive. No matter what Jim did, King would just open up like a book and let Jim enjoy him, no matter the sexual experience. Jim had a long and thick dick that King just loved to ravage. When Jim attacked King's manhole, whimpers and screams of elation could be heard all over the house.

This was King's way of turning off and relaxing. He went from being mean and controlling to incredibly affectionate and docile. Mentally, Jim thought about how King had killed and maimed so many people, yet he enjoyed being passive to balance his aggressive nature while living the gang life. Jim treated him like a slut in bed, and King loved it.

King told Jim one night that he would kill him if he ever told anybody about their sexual encounters. Jim understood the warning clearly. "No one will ever know about it – not even Ron."

When Jim was getting ready to leave, Jim said that his business could need his gang's help. He told King that his company wanted to control all import/export firms in the Caribbean.

"There's going to be a criminal element to it, and everybody on board the Tito III's will be in danger. Could you call upon your gang to provide some muscle if we need help?"

King replied with a smile, "Money always talks."

"How much of a retainer do you need upfront; I'm going to tell you now there will probably be some real dirty dealings, and we may even need some hits."

King thought for a few seconds and said, "$100,000 US dollars monthly plus an extra fee for each job."

"You're hired. What do you want me to do with the $100,000?"

"I only deal in cash."

Jim asked if it would be okay if he had one of his boys bring it to him tomorrow. King gave Jim an address on a piece of paper and said deliver it there.

"Call me when the cash is going to arrive. Also, send me a picture of the delivery guy and his name."

"No problem."

Everything was signed and sealed. Jim left King's house thinking, *well, that was a fucking productive day.*

Ron made his rounds contacting their three competitors, and so far, only one company was receptive to their $225 million cash offer. They now are the proud owners of Lopez Shipping, and the former owner Jesus Lopez was more than a happy camper with this deal. They all decided that they would assign Lopez Shipping to Butch's operation in Jamaica. They gave him a call and told him to expect Lopez shipping containers and some of its employees for it's now under his Jamaican import/export authority. Ron told Butch that if he had any issues, he knew his phone number.

The next two competitors were Trans-Pac shipping and CMA shipping. Both refused Ron's offer to buy them out, so Ron turned them over to Jim. Jim made a quick phone call to King and told him that he had two problems for him to solve.

"We've got two shipping companies that don't want to sell in Panama and Venezuela. Can you be of any assistance?"

King replied, "Yes, I have resources at each location, and you will hear from the shipping companies shortly, and I'm sure they will be more than happy to accept your offer."

"Let me know what I owe you."

"I'll get back to you on that; I think there are some other forms of payment rather than the cash that we can negotiate." Jim hung up in bewilderment, wondering when that negotiation was going to take place.

Ron and Jim sat down and went over the research they conducted on the two remaining companies. Trans-Pac shipping was in Panama, and based upon its shipping manifest, a majority of the containers have one primary shipper, "El Chapo." An interesting fact about "El Chapo" was that he was one of our primary shippers out of Panama, Guatemala, and Venezuela. It appears that his cargo is so large that he had to split it up among several ports.

CMA shipping was located in Venezuela. It handled all of the shipments for Carlos Lehder (Columbia's most feared drug Lord) in addition to shipments for El Chapo. The transition between shippers must be handled delicately so as not to raise any red flags.

The next day Ron got a call from both shipping offices that they were ready to accept our offer. Ron finalized all the paperwork, and the money transfers were completed. The next phone call that Ron made was to Jamison in Venezuela. He told him that he now had two of the most notorious drug lords, Carlos Lehder and El Chapo, doing business through his office. They were shipping a massive number of containers to various destinations on the East Coast of the United States and Europe. He was instructed to keep everything operating smoothly, particularly with these shipments.

Ron, Jim, and David met in the man cave. They began to plot their goals now that they owned everything in the Caribbean, including all of the import/export ports and seven yacht clubs on several islands strategically placed throughout the Caribbean. They had spent an enormous amount of capital reserve and taken on a large amount of debt. Now they had to put a plan together to start increasing their service charges a small percentage at a time. This would most likely happen without much notice from all their shippers.

That night Jim dominated Ron more aggressively than he was not used to. In Jim and King's sexual encounters, Jim dominated King so aggressively that King just surrendered like a little girl lusting for pleasure. Tonight Ron was introduced to Jim's dark side and found it excitingly enjoyable. When Ron and Jim had finished showering after their sloppy night of sadomasochistic sex, they heard a knocking at the door. It was David.

"Can I come in and sit for a while?"

Still wrapped in their towels, they let David through as he sat at the foot of their bed. David said that he wanted to spend the night with them because he was very concerned about their safety and quite scared himself.

"It feels like we're getting into something that we're not ready to handle. I don't have any experience shooting people like they do. I never was in the military, nor even went hunting. The ways things are looking, I fear that it may come down to it."

Jim spoke up, "David, that's what you have me for. We've worked alongside each other for over seven years, and we've always protected you." With a smile, David moved in between Ron and Jim, who took their towels off, and for the first time, David saw their fully nude bodies. The expression on his face was one of total disbelief because Ron and Jim stood there like the chiseled statues of David right in front of his eyes. They were so beautiful in his eyes that his erection could not be hidden anymore.

He put his arms around them, drawing them inwards while his erect penis throbbed even harder. Jim looked into David's eyes and said: "Our love has a boundary, are you sure you want to cross it"? David looked into Ron's eyes for approval. Ron shook his head in disapproval.

David replied, "Our friendship has more power and love than any relationship I have ever had. I don't want to destroy it. I know for sure now that both of you will protect me." David kissed them both on the cheek and returned to his room. Jim thanked Ron for respecting their relationship with David, curled up with their arms around one another, and then went to sleep.

The next morning, Jim telephoned King, letting him know that another mission may soon be in the works if he was up for it. They were going to dock off an isolated island about twenty-five miles from Jamaica, so they would be close. Jim had some strategizing to do concerning their business, and they needed the peace and tranquility of the open sea to influence their decisions. They would have a leisurely anchor at the island for a couple of days and be back in Jamaica on Friday.

Simon and Adam were on constant patrol covering the 130'. It was five-thirty in the evening, well into the cocktail time, and the alarm system went off, indicating a watercraft's presence within a hundred-mile radius. Simon and Adam immediately proceeded to the Captain's deck to analyze the situation and told the others to stay put. Over the PA system, Simon announced two "cigarette boats" are approaching at a blaring 80 knots (92 MPH) from the port side and would be upon us in about fifty minutes. Jim immediately telephoned King and told him to dispatch his men to our yacht and described the situation's urgency. During the conversation, he gave King the coordinates of their location.

Simon issued every person on board a MK 23 handgun along with an AK-47. Adam and Simon always carried a MK 23, so all they had to pick up was their HK MP5 along with an M249 5.56mm light machine gun (LMG). Even though they had a complete arsenal of weapons and explosives at their disposal, they deeded the situation at hand called for the guns to be issued to the entire crew. Everybody on board knew their designated positions and reported to them. Simon mounted his LMG at the front of the yacht while Adam mounted his in the back. Now they played the waiting game. They purposely put David on the highest point on the yacht behind bulletproof glass with a little opening for him to shoot out of, but he served as more of a lookout. They had practiced their emergency attack formation several times and hoped that they would never have to put it into action. Jim prayed that David was okay with the routine.

Captain John told Jim that King was on the phone for him. Jim ran to the control room and explained the situation they were currently in with the cigarette boats approaching within the next ten minutes.

"It appears that pirates are on the way; our lookout indicated that they are coming heavily armed with what looks to be rifles and possibly a grenade or rocket launcher on one of the boats," King reported.

"King, we need to eliminate this threat as soon as possible. Hire whatever launchers or go-boats that you need and get out here right away." Then Jim repeated the latitude and longitude of their location.

"On my way, ETA – seven minutes."

Just then, all hell broke loose. You heard the booming cracks from Simon and Adam's LMGs, the roaring of engines, and the pitter-patter of machine-gun fire hitting the yacht from bow to stern. The bulletproof windows were being tested at all levels on the yacht. The cigarette boats seem to dance around the LMG fire as they inched closer. What they didn't know was that Simon and Adam were leading them into their kill zone where their weapons would be most effective. Suddenly Simon and Adam began to let loose a barrage of gunfire at one boat, sinking it instantly. Adam then ran to the boat's bow with his MP5, aimed the second boat as it passed him, and hit it with an onslaught of rounds that ignited the gas tank, and it blew up. The boats' survivors were bobbing around in the water and were to be taken in as hostages.

While Simon was still in his position on the yacht's stern, he noticed two launches coming in from the north and loaded and cocked back his LMG. Just then, Jim received a call from King telling him that his forces would be there any second. Jim alerted Simon that the launches that were coming in were friendly and sent by King to assist in our attempted takeover.

While they waited for the launches to arrive, they left the pirates to bob in the ocean. When the launches arrived, its leader boarded the yacht, and they told him that they wanted to take the pirates in and interrogate them to find out who initiated the attack. He said, " We'll take 'em back to port, and I'll guarantee we'll find out who did it. As the pirates were loaded onto the launches to be taken back, Jim called King and thanked him for his help. He told him that the surviving pirates are now on their way back to Jamaica, and he wanted to know who was behind their attack. King assured Jim that it would be his pleasure to extract the information out of them.

About 10 a.m., two days later, Jim got a phone call from King. Of the seven survivors, they had made it down to the last two of them before they started talking. The threat originated in Guatemala. The hostages didn't know how far up the chain of command that order came from but knew an associate of the Eric "Little El Capo" Salvador of the El Capo Cartel made the call. Jim thanked King and asked him if he would like to come over to the yacht for dinner when they got back to port? Surprisingly, King graciously accepted.

When they got back to port in Jamaica, Captain John had the yacht refitted while Simon had the boat gone over from bow to stern, ensuring no bullet holes caused any significant damage. Jim called King and invited him to dinner on Tuesday night.

After King accepted the dinner invitation, Jim met with Simon, Adam, Ron, and David. He explained to them about King's gang operation in the Caribbean. He wanted them to know that he was on their side and on a monthly retainer to provide extra security services. He could be trusted to be called upon and to perform any illegal activity anywhere in the Caribbean. His cutthroat tactics are well known, and he is feared without exception. They are fortunate to have him on their team. Of course, everything and everyone comes at a cost.

King arrived on time with his complement of security guards. The yacht was parked at an obscure location in the Royal Jamaican Yacht Club, so his arrival did not cause any unusual activity on the dock. Ron had never met King; the only thing he knew was that Jim had a sexual relationship with him to get additional security for the Tito III. To Ron's surprise, King's appearance and small stature was anything but threatening. He wondered how this little man became so powerful and the leader of such a notoriously cutthroat gang.

That night, the three of them enjoyed an exquisite dinner of prime rib, garlic mashed potatoes, asparagus with small white onions, and a chocolate mousse for dessert. King asked as to the name of their chef. Jim summoned Chef Timothy to the dining room, where he was introduced to King and received his five-star review.

King got up out of his chair, shook Timothy's hand, and said, "I've never had a better meal in my life. He then went on to say that they have such an exquisite staff on this yacht. Where did you find this fine collection of men?"

Ron replied, "This crew came from another boat that had sold at the same time they purchased this yacht. We hired all of them at once because they had worked together for over five years and are a well-oiled team, and they're all completely gay. It keeps our lives on the yacht interesting."

After dinner, they all retreated to the salon, where they had after-dinner drinks. King took a particular fancy to Stephen, as he was his primary server. He made comments as to Stephan's masculinity. After a couple of drinks, King asked if he could get a tour of the yacht?

Jim said, "Most assuredly, just follow me." When Jim stepped inside the master suite, King shut the door behind them with a bang."

"It's been far too long, Jim, I've missed you."

Jim didn't know what to say. Finally, he said, "King, you know Ron's onboard, and I would be very uncomfortable doing anything on the yacht."

"Why don't you asked Ron to join us?" Jim thought to himself that this was a bad idea all the way around. He didn't know how Ron would react to this situation.

King said, "I'll ask him."

"Okay, go ahead."

When Ron appeared in the master suite, he had no idea what was going on. As King did before, as soon as Ron walked in, he gave it a big slam. Then he smiled and said, "You guys... how would you like to ravish me with your dominance?"

Jim looked at Ron and proceeded to take his clothes off just as King was doing. When Jim and King were both naked and spread out on the oversized bed, Ron slowly started to get undressed. To Jim's surprise, when Ron was fully naked, he stood erect and ready for action. Together Ron and Jim ravished King from head to toe. They put him in such forced penetration positions that he howled even more of his usual sounds of pleasure.

Ron had never been with a black man before. King's body was beautiful to the touch and smell, his dick was quite massive for his size, and he thoroughly enjoyed the entire event. While all of this was going on with King, Ron and Jim had exquisite sex. Ron attacked Jim's manhole with such passion that when Jim's erect dick plunged into King, all three climaxed simultaneously. They had all achieved the ultimate orgasm and laid out on the bed panting with exhausted pleasure.

"I thoroughly enjoyed this, Jim; I didn't realize you had such a gingerly mate," King said as all three of them got dressed and returned to the main salon. Soon after, King, escorted by his security detail, left the dock on his way home.

After everything was all over, Jim and Ron sat on the back deck to discuss that night's events. Ron was first to speak up, saying how he enjoyed tonight. He continued, "Now I know what you and King have been doing. It's kind of fascinating, isn't it, dominating such a powerful man. Can you imagine how many people he has killed or maimed, but tonight we both ravaged him like he was our bitch?"

"Whatever it takes to keep him on our team," replied Jim.

Ron continued, "I didn't realize all of the dangers that we were exposed to while I was purchasing the yacht harbors and import/export companies. You did, Jim, and you did what you had to do to secure our safety. I appreciate the degree you will go to protect all of us, and I will do my part, too. I want to ensure our relationship with King is protected."

In total amazement, Jim sat there and thanked Ron for his understanding and acceptance but most of all for participating in tonight's sexual bliss.

The following morning Ron, Jim, and David were in the office recapping the prior night's events with King. They were impressed with how quickly his organization had convinced the last two shipping companies to sell. Ron suggested that Jim find out which ports in the Caribbean that King's organization control. Jim agreed that he would contact King and get the information.

That afternoon Jim gave King a call and told him that they had import/export companies in Jamaica, Grand Caymans, Panama, Guatemala, and Venezuela. He asked if King had resources in all of these ports where they conduct business. He replied the only one that they don't have a connection with is Panama.

"We have the support of the "Black Disciples Gang in Panama." They provide us support there, and we assist them in Jamaica. It's a perfect trade-off."

"But, I'd like to speak off the record about the Black Disciples. They're led by three brothers, two gay and one bisexual. When we made arrangements for our partnership in Panama and Jamaica, I had to have a four-way to seal the deal. Leroy, the oldest brother, said they always seal a deal with sex because that way, they cannot be blackmailed. It's widely known within their organization that the leaders are gay, but no one has ever disclosed a sexual relationship with them. Be assured that if someone did, they'd be executed on the spot. The Black Disciples are notorious killers and a gang not to be underestimated."

Jim reported to Ron and David that King's organization, assisted by another gang, would have all of their ports-of-call covered, so it was time to make some serious plans to form their Cartel. They all agreed that their skills were adequate to manage a cartel operation, and they needed an organization that would be lethal and loyal to their cartel. Ron brought up the idea of offering King a 15% interest in their overall net profit to be a partner in their business. They want to buy King's unconditional loyalty to the Marquis Cartel. Jim and Ron agreed with Ron's idea.

Jim contacted King and ask him to come to the yacht because they had some business to discuss. When King arrived, they all went to the man cave for drinks, and King's inquisitive mind was waiting for the big announcement forthcoming. Jim went over their cartel's need for the resources that King's organization can provide.

"We're prepared to offer you fifteen percent of our net profit monthly for King to become a silent partner in RJD, LLC. Our current monthly net profit is ten million dollars, so your share would be $1.5 million."

King stood up and said he'd honored to be on Ron, Jim, and David's team. He went on to say, "This is the first time I've ever felt like I have an actual family to protect. I just love you guys. Now let's have some fun, get and make a hell of a lot of money."

Ron laughed and responded, "With your help, King, we can make a lot more money, so have your team prepared to go to battle. They are going to shake the bushes and make some changes around here."

POWERHOUSE

$\mathcal{J}$im went on to notify all of their port managers to schedule their cargo ships' arrival three days late to the port. In doing so, the cartels' outgoing cargo will be delayed, and it will impact their cash flow. When the port managers asked about the delay, they were told to say that new management has raised the export fees by 25%. When those fees are paid, the ships will again arrive on their normal schedule. The managers reported back to Jim that they received a lot of very forceful angry feedback such as: "Do you know who you're doing business with"? Jim told every port manager that a security detail has been dispatched to their location and would arrive shortly.

"The Black Disciples will guard our ports in Panama," Jim told Alex, "They are led by three brothers Leroy, Lloyd, and Devon – two are gay, and one is bisexual. They generally make sexual demands with anyone they work with, so I just wanted to give you a heads up."

Alex replied, "I'll be looking forward to it; it's been a long dry spell here in Panama." It didn't take long after Alex was warned of their sexual advances that the three brothers showed up at his office door with a big smile on their face. They introduced themselves and suggested that the four of them have dinner together that night. Alex confirmed their invitation and recommended that they dine at his hotel at the Panama City yacht club. Leroy confirmed that the three of them would be there at 7 o'clock.

Jim had warned Alex as to the three brothers' need for sexual validation of every new client. He placed a call to Captain John to ask what he had heard about this gang. John said he had not been in any meetings that Jim or Ron had held concerning that gang. King, the leader of the notorious Jamaican gang, was on board recently for dinner. Alex was left to manage the dinner and the night of entertainment on his own. Leroy and his brothers had rented a suite at the club for a few days, and he was invited to their suite after dinner. Once inside the suite, Leroy and Lloyd disappeared into one of the bedrooms while Devon and Alex made cocktails from their bar.

Without fanfare, the two brothers reappeared nude and joined them at the bar. Alex was astounded that Leroy and Lloyd's bodies looked like they were twins. They were both about 6'1", a delightful chocolate brown, six-pack frame, hairy naval down to their pubic switch. It was robust with black hair that surrounded an enviable, uncut piece of manhood. Alex stood there in a state of readiness. He was waiting for them to attack. It was Devon who started to undress him. Every piece of his clothing was folded neatly and placed on the chair next to the bar.

Within seconds he stood there totally naked in front of his guests. They lead Alex into the master suite, where Leroy and Lloyd started to please themselves with his black-hair covered body. When Leroy and Lloyd had Alex in a state of sexual bliss, Devon joined in, and he and Leroy double penetrated Alex, who let out a moan that could probably be heard in the hallway of the yacht club.

When they were all dressed, and Alex was ready to depart, Lloyd spoke up and said, "It's a pleasure to be working with you. Our gang numbers over a hundred strong and will ensure your safety at all times. Thank you for a beautiful evening; let's do it again. You can always recognize our gang members because they wear a white bandanna around their forehead while they're patrolling your location. They will also be in earshot at the yacht club, so please rest assured that you're being protected at all times."

Alex said good night and headed to his room, only five doors away. Once inside, he stripped off all of his clothes and jumped in the shower, soaking his manhole in steaming water, hoping to reduce his pain and suffering.

In an unbelievably short period, Jim and his team have mastered the operational control of all of the export/import cargo moving in the Caribbean Sea and the Gulf Coast of Central America from Venezuela to Panama. They now received 25% additional fees and were known as the "Marquis Cartel," in partnership with the King Cartel and the Black Disciples Cartel in Panama.

Jim's method of operation had changed dramatically. He not only is outstanding at communication, operations, directing, and controlling, but he has also developed King's mercenary tactics. Like King, he hired two personal bodyguards and now had a direct line of communication throughout King's organization, starting from his lieutenants to line sergeants. At any time, Jim could make a phone call and quickly solve a situation.

Cartel operations were at 100%. Ron's birthday was approaching, and Jim was bewildered as to what to buy him.

We have everything we want. Hmm... What about a new yacht! This 130'er is just too small. Since we brought on those two bodyguards, anyone else will not have a real place to stay. If we bring aboard more than our staff, everyone else would have to sleep on a sofa bed or cot onboard. It's time we upgrade from the Tito III. It's seen a lot of wear and tear, and it is time for a new toy. It's time they get a bigger master suite for whenever King comes over... with him, we need all the room we can get.

Jim did his due diligence on yacht builders. He chose FEADSHIP Yacht Builders in the Netherlands, for they have been in business since the 1890s and their yachts are the most prized in the world. He called the company and made an appointment to fly in to meet with them the following week. On the next Tuesday morning, around 10 o'clock, Jim arrived at the yacht yard and met with Jake Goldsmith, one of the company's owners. He went into Jake's office, which was lavishly appointed with various custom-made yacht furnishings. Jim came right out and said, "I'm looking for a new 150' foot yacht."

"Don't you want one custom-built?"

"No," Jim replied, "my partner's birthday is in less than a month, and I want to surprise him with it. So, when can we get this search started?"

Jake shook his head and said, "We have four 150' yachts in the yard. They are all destined for different sales yards. All of the yachts had one common factor. They had seven staterooms that slept fourteen guests, each with private baths and crew rooms that accommodate a crew of ten, including the Captain. They just have a different design, coloring, carpet, wood, and electronic equipment. They're all for sale, would you like to take a look at them?"

"Yes, immediately," Jim replied.

It took three days for Jim to review all of the yachts in detail, always comparing their shortcomings and value-added features. They felt like home when you walked onboard with their rich mahogany wood and accent color tones. This yacht design was for the more pristine in class, not the younger party group. The yacht had four decks; the top one would be the captain's bridge, and the one below would house the office, man cave, and Jim and Ron's master suite. The next deck down would be a bar, game and TV room, den, and back deck to relax. The bottom deck would have the galley, dining room, master salon, covered dining area on the back deck, and the back deck's uncovered seating area. Further ahead on that floor were two master suites.

Of course, all bedrooms on the yacht had their private baths. There was room for a crew of ten, including the captain quarters and private staterooms for fourteen guests sleeping double occupancy.

Jake said, "I think I've got just the yacht for you." They jumped a golf cart and went to a yacht that was in dry dock. They climbed up several steps and boarded the back deck of the vessel. As Jim walked through the ship, he was in awe. The wood was not mahogany; it looked as if it was must be African Blackwood.

Jake turned to Jim and said, "Yes… That's real Blackwood. The yacht's furnishings looked as if they were specially made for Ron, David, and Jim. Ornate construction but firmly built with plush padding to extenuate each piece's richness. It was all and more than he asked for. The second-floor office just below the bridge was beautiful with the 360° panoramic view of the water, that is, if it was setting in water. Everything seemed almost too perfect to be true.

Jim said, "When can I take it for a test drive?"

"We'll get it in the water as soon as possible."

The next afternoon Jim was at the helm of the 150' foot yacht. He glided it out of the harbor and hit it full throttle to the open sea. It responded beautifully to the two Caterpillar C18 engines as he maneuvered the craft for about three hours and then circled and headed back into the harbor.

He told Jake, "If I can dock it, I'll buy it."

As Jim pulled into the yacht yard, he decided which side-tie that he needed to move the yacht alongside. He slowly set his thrusters to 10° and proceeded with a light reverse on the starboard engine. Docking is a slow and tedious process one never rushes. Jim slowly pulled the boat into perfect position as the deckhands threw the lines overboard, and the dockhands secured the lines.

Jake said, "It looks like we've got a deal."

All that was left now was to negotiate the sales price of $110 million US Dollars. Jim said, "$85 million out the door, and I'll take it as it is today. No modifications, no changes, I want it shipped to Grand Cayman yacht club immediately. I'll wire you five million dollars now, and the rest when the yacht is delivered to the Grand Caymans." Take it or leave it.

Jake said, "I'll take it if it's all-cash."

Jim said, "No problem, I'll have five million dollars in cash here this afternoon." He placed a call to David to have him wire five million dollars in cash to him in the Netherlands and specified the bank closest to the yacht yard. Within the hour, Jim got a phone call from the bank that the money was ready to be picked up.

That evening, over cocktails in Jake's office, RJD and K, LLC were now proud owners of a new 150' yacht. Jim called Ron to initiate the paperwork necessary to register the yacht, and sales papers were faxed to his office that evening. Jim told Ron not to ask any questions, just to prepare the paperwork and file it. After the third round of drinks, Jake asked who Jim's lover was.

Jim responded, "His name is Ron, and we've been together for about fourteen years. Do you have a problem with that?"

Jake said, "No, it's just unusual for a couple such as yourselves to buy such an expensive yacht. I haven't had a customer like you before."

Jim was quick to reply, " Do you mean someone with money or gay?"

Jake was left kind of on the spot, but he answered, "Yes, gay."

Jim laughed, "I bet you had quite a few gay customers in your past, and you just didn't know it. You shouldn't be too concerned, Jake, money talks, bull shit walks."

They delivered the yacht to the Grand Cayman yacht club in ten days. On his arrival, Jim went to his safe in the office and withdrew the remaining money needed to close the deal in cash ($80 Million). At that point, Jim did not concern himself about the amount of money going through the US banking system to buy the vessel. He didn't want to run it through the company account because Ron would see it, and it wouldn't be a surprise anymore. So, all the final paperwork was signed and sealed by him alone.

That evening Jim took David, Simon, Adam, and King to see the new yacht. They were exuberant over the décor, the number of staterooms, the lavish office, and the yacht's total layout and furnishings. Simon immediately scheduled a refitting, and David would be responsible for transferring all the electronics. Chef Tim took care of the necessary cooking supplies and pantry items. Andrew and Stephen were responsible for moving all of Ron, Jim and David's personnel items. Simon and Adam were to take care of the yachts floating arsenal and their items. The new name of the yacht will be the Tito IV.

Tito, killed in Vietnam decades ago, lives on through Jim, in the Martinez Empire. With the help of Jim, Ron, and David, and now with King, it has grown to control the import/export business in all of the Caribbean Sea and the gulf coast of Central America from Venezuela to Panama. Ron's birthday was now only a few days away.

'Where are we going to have the party?" he asked David.

David thought a minute and said, "How about that island we always go to and tie-up. It is nice and secluded, and it would hold hundreds of us."

Jim asked Ron to find out who owns that island that they always tie-up on 25 miles from Miami.

Ron asked, " Why?"

Jim said, "I thought that it might be another nice addition to our portfolio." Ron got back to Jim and told him the name of the island's owner – someone with a foreign-sounding name that was too hard to pronounce or remember. Jim had Ron write up a proposal to purchase the amount and immediately send it to the owner in Miami.

They did not get a reply to their offer, so Ron called the island owner and inquired if they received it.

He said, "Yes, I'm not interested in selling." And then he hung up the phone.

Jim called King, described the situation, and that he wanted to buy the island. He asked if King could take care of it, please. He also suggested that King come over for dinner, for they had not seen him in a while and missed him.

King jumped at the invitation, "I'll be there tonight!"

Jim said, "I will be looking for you to show up anytime." That night Jim had Ron sent a new offer to purchase the island for twenty-five million dollars, including all mineral rights, water rights, and sea rights. Two days later, they signed real estate documents with a note that said everything would be finalized by tonight. Jim called King and thanked him for the fast work.

King laughed and said, "You want to see some fast work; I'll show you some tonight." Jim hung up with a big smile on his face fantasizing about the night to come.

Jim asked David to send out party invitations for Ron's birthday at the island, beginning at two in the afternoon on his birthday Saturday and ending Sunday at 3 PM.

"Come one, come all, and have a good time for my husband, Ron's birthday."

This was the first time either one of them had "come out" in a public event. "I wonder what's going to come out of this," Jim asked. David and Jim had a clear understanding that everybody going to the party would have to have a yacht or some type of watercraft.

At least that would provide shelter for them. David called a porta potty company to deliver thirty executive porta potty's and five showers units. David made the next call to "The Caterers to the Yachts," their old standby catering firm, and gave them instructions to fill the yacht's pantry and refrigerator and freezer with ample supplies for three days and fifty people on board.

Next, Jim had a meeting with Simon, Adam, and King to discuss security at the island event. Simon brought up that all attendees need to be cleared before they attend the party.

"We have to be concerned about our arriving motor craft. The first problem is how to clear everybody coming on the island?" Simon questioned.

Adam replied, "We can set up a buffer zone around the island, like a quarter-mile zone. Nobody crosses that quarter-mile zone until their yachts or vessels are checked by our security detail. Whether it's our crew, King's crew, or the Black Disciples, nobody can pass that checkpoint. If they cross it without clearance, we open fire. No exceptions. We should communicate this warning to every vessel going to the island."

Jim felt that everything was ready for Ron's big birthday bash. He was so excited to welcome him aboard his present, the Tito IV, and then taking him to his second present, the new island headquarters for the Marquis Cartel. His little birthday cost a minimum of 135 million in cash.

Jim laughed, "Well, my safe is almost empty. I better get to work."

A mass co-mingling of all of the gangs of Miami, Panama, and parts unknown attended Ron's birthday party. At any given time, you could see pearl-handled 45s, diamond-studded revolvers, guys with red, white, and blue bandannas, all having a good time on the Marquis Cartel's island.

As the night progressed, so did the drunkenness. The macho gangsters were intertwined with their pants down around their ankles, going at it like dogs in heat. They didn't care because it was an all-male party, and on this deserted island where no one, except the family, could attend. This place is a well-guarded secret. Fireworks erupted while Jim and Ron both shared a drink, admiring all that they have accomplished with each other.

The night led to morning, and mimosas were flowing until noon. Chef Tim set out a spread for everyone on board, and they ate and ate until they could not eat anymore. The three new crew members worked quite well with Captain John and the rest of the crew. They were hired due to the extra demands of the larger yacht size and the additional quarters and living spaces' upkeep. The new crew hands were:

Addison stands 5'10" and sports black straight hair with bangs. He is half native American. This is his second yacht assignment; the last one was a 70'er. He is assigned to stateroom duty and laundry full-time.

Irwin is 5'7" with long blonde hair, a bodybuilder's physique and sexy blue eyes. He is charmingly graceful and is assigned to the living quarters, salon detail full-time, and a server at meals.

Baron is the tallest at 5'11". A handsome black man, he has closely cut curly hair, is slender, and always has an enthusiastic smile. "Yes, sir," "No, sir," to every request. The Tito IV is his first yacht. He is assigned to stateroom duty and work alongside Addison.

With the complement of our original team, they ran the entire yacht. With only seven crew members, this might seem a massive undertaking. However, with a ratio of seven crew to only three owners living onboard, everything should run smoothly. It's a brand-new yacht, so they are not anticipating any operational problems. If there are any, the yacht company will have to send a manufacturer representative to fix it. Captain John has run the yacht through its paces and found it extremely responsive and fast for a yacht of its size.

On Wednesday after Ron's birthday, Jim had Captain John charter a course for Panama. It was time to visit their associates, the Black Disciples and port manager, Alex. They planned to take a leisurely trip from the Grand Caymans to the Panama Yacht Club in Panama City, Panama.

When they were out of port, past Jamaica, in what they call the *no man's land*, storm warnings alerted them that an enormous category four hurricane changed course and was coming in from the south, southeast. All watercraft in our general area were advised to shelter in place and batten down the hatches. At this point, there was no place to go to outrun it.

Captain John sounded the ship's alarm. All the staff and crew gathered in the man cave and waited for further instructions until he arrived and gave them the bad news. They were in the direct path of a hurricane that would be upon them soon, with no place to run. He would maneuver the yacht facing the eye of the storm, and the crew should ensure that all hatches are shut and all doors securely fastened. All watertight doorways need to be secured as quickly as possible so the yacht would not take on water and sink. Life vests were to be worn at all times. The best place for everyone to ride out the storm would be in the main saloon. It's well protected by three decks above and two decks below. You can escape through both side doors and the back sliding-glass door.

Jim remembered when he was at the shipyards, and Jake referenced something about stabilizer bars during rough seas. He called Captain John on the intercom and told him to check the manual about stabilizers during rough seas. Captain John then told him that they can activate hydraulic stabilizer bars to extend thirty-feet out on each side of the boat to stabilize it when navigating rough seas.

Captain John said, "That's a lifesaver; I'll extend the stabilizer bars immediately." As soon as the bars were set, the yacht began to feel as if it was sailing through the water. It was like skipping through the water on each rough wave.

With each passing wave, the yacht dropped a little further down as the size of the waves increased. Everyone on board braced themselves as they watched anything that was not bolted down roll across the floor. Jim watched his favorite pen disappear into the mess and wondered just how bad it would get.

This is going to be hell to clean.

The winds grew more potent, and their howl could be heard even in what normally is considered a soundproof room. The forceful wind gust and rogue waves rocked the yacht incessantly, sending anyone who was not sitting and bracing themselves to the floor. This battering seemed to last forever when suddenly, the Captain's voice boomed over the intercom.

"Within thirty minutes, the eye of the storm will be upon us, and there will be an ultimately quiet period until we cross into the outer wall of the storm. We're almost halfway through it, and the yacht is handling it as well as a boat twice its size."

When the outer wall hit, the turbulence was vicious and knocked everyone to their feet. They rolled around the saloon floor like popcorn in a hot skillet. One wave engulfed the entire yacht but quickly passed. After what seemed like days, Captain John set the yacht to full throttle and headed out of the storm to calmer waters.

Soon after, Captain John slowed to an idle and assessed any damage to the TITO IV. Ron, who thought he had already earned his sea legs, told Jim, "Let's never do this again." Jim looked at Ron and laughed. Then he looked around his once pristine yacht and sighed. They had a mess to clean up before they could set sail again. David, who was seasick the entire time, looked at Jim and said, "Take me to land any land... I'm not picky; as long as it has dirt and doesn't move, I'll be fine."

THE JUDAS KISS

*H*ow far away are we from the Panama All Yacht Club?" Jim asked Captain John.

"Only about forty-five minutes.

Jim got on the phone with who he thought was the harbormaster, informing him that the Tito IV would arrive shortly and have one of the 150' slips ready for their arrival. Jim also requested that the dock boys be dispatched to the slip as soon as possible. After that, he called Alex to tell him that they were getting ready to tie up on Dock 2.

Perplexed, Alex questioned, "How did you know which dock to tie up at, and how did you get your dock boys?

Jim replied, "I just called the harbormaster who gave us our dock assignment and had dockhands ready to catch our lines."

Alex said, "There should never be any direct communication with the harbormaster. He knows this protocol, which is for your privacy and protection." The Tito IV's arrival has now been announced to the world, and there is no secret that the Marquis Cartel is now in town.

Hearing the news, Leroy, Lloyd, and Devon broke away from their usual duties and headed right down to the Tito IV. Everyone knew that its position had been compromised and was currently docked in Panama City. This yacht carried all the movers and the shaker of the Marquis Cartel. They had to get out of Panama and fast. Captain John gave the orders to untie the yacht and motored silently to the next deep channel port, where he backed in and made a left turn for the open sea. Leroy got on the radio with the Captain and told him that he had clearance for Tito IV to dock at a marina three-quarters of a mile down the coastline, on the starboard side. One of the Black Disciple's fast boats would pull alongside the yacht and escort them to the secluded yacht harbor. Just then, a man in another speedboat pulled up alongside the Tito IV and motioned the captain to follow him. The slip that they were going into is for 290' side ties, which over-accommodated the Tito IV but leaves enough room at either end for a fast boat to be secured as well.

Jim thanked Leroy for going all-out to protect him and his crew in Panama. Jim then called King, telling him what had transpired, and asked if he could make it down there tomorrow.

"I would feel a lot safer knowing you're around."

King was delighted to hear that and said he'd arrive sometime in the afternoon. After his call, Jim invited Alex, Lloyd, Devon, and Leroy to dinner that night to catch up on what's been going on in Panama and to have some good old-fashioned fun. Chef Tim prepared an outstanding spread of grilled salmon, baked sweet potatoes, asparagus, and angel food cake with strawberries for dessert. While kicking it in the man cave, all seven of them had a little bit too much to drink. David had a good time with the group, but when it came time for any sexual activity, he quietly excused himself and went below for the remainder of the evening.

Now that there were six of them left in the man cave, the pairing off began. Leroy was a notorious top, Lloyd was a power bottom, and Devon was open to any position. Jim grabbed Lloyd and escorted him to one of the private rooms downstairs. Leroy grabbed Ron's arm, gave him a big hug and a kiss, and they disappeared into the suite behind the man cave. Alex, Captain Ron's ex, was completely versatile; he grabbed Devon and took him to the back deck. The evening continued as imagined, all having quite a pleasurable time and further securing their association with the Black Disciples.

When morning came, they all appeared at the main dining table at about 9 o'clock. Irwin and Andrew served mimosas all the way around, and after about an hour, he laid out a breakfast that Chef Timothy had so meticulously prepared. As Jim strolled up to the office, he had a 360° view through the windows that revealed his security guards posted at strategic points throughout the marina. There must've been at least twenty-five to thirty gangsters at their beck and call. The feeling was nice.

Ron, Jim, and David met with Alex to go over port operations and any concerns about security and payments for shipments. He said, "The Black Disciples are providing the best security that I've ever seen. As for payments, there is only one shipper that's slow on their payments."

Jim inquired as to who they were. "They call him "El Capo," an up and coming hotshot from Guatemala."

"How far behind is he in his payments," Jim asked.

"He owes us $750,000 for the last ninety days. I've held up his shipments until he pays. Word on the street is that there's a lot of tension about us holding up his exports, so they're keeping a close eye on Guatemala."

While they were in the office, Jim got a call from one of the security guards on his payroll. He said that ten armored cars had just arrived and recently received passage through and are now heading for the inner harbor where the Tito IV is docked. Jim asked the guard if he could estimate the number of gangsters that were heading in his direction. The guard estimated that each vehicle could hold at least eight to ten gangsters, so about a hundred men are on their way to attack the yacht. Jim let out a warning over the PA systems requesting "all hands on deck." Instantly everyone on board reported to the office, and Simon and Leroy began their contingency plan. Leroy placed a call to four of his lieutenants, which rounded up at least two hundred of their men to report to the dock as soon as possible. In the meantime, Simon had everyone on the yacht heavily armed and in their battle station. They didn't know exactly what was going to happen, but they were sure it would be quite a show.

Leroy was the first to sound the alarm. He received a call from one of his lieutenants that an enormous number of cartel gangsters had encircled the harbor. Strategically speaking, their best defensive measure would be to utilize their smaller and more agile fast boats to escort the yacht out of the harbor. Captain John had his crew throw the lines on the tie-up dock so that he could navigate out of the harbor as fast as possible. One fast boat preceded the yacht, and the other fast boat escorted the yacht alongside. When they got to the harbor's opening just before hitting the sea, all hell broke loose. Machine-gun fire came from all directions on the docks.

The harbor entrance was like a horseshoe bottlenecked at the end, so Captain John had to navigate through a small opening heavily fortified by the cartel. Everyone onboard armed with assault rifles returned fire. Simon and Adam stationed both of the yacht's heavy machine guns up front. They began the 50-caliber assault on the enemy encampment in an attempt to eliminate hostile gunfire as the yacht tried to depart the harbor.

Jim was on the starboard side on the third deck, Ron on the port, both armed with light machine guns and returning fire on all who moved. They had the advantage of being in a slightly higher position than the enemy, and boy did they make them pay. Their Vietnam days had served them well, for they were no rookies to gunfire and their unflinching nerve matched with their precise aim helped thin out the lines that surrounded them. Not accustomed to war, David ran supply duties, feeding them all with ammunition and occasionally giving suppressive fire with his AK-47.

Suddenly, a large explosion hit the water ten feet from the boat's port side, drenching both Ron and Simon with water. Simon shouted, "They must have stopped trying to take the boat and are planning to sink it! Watch for rockets!" One of the speed boats took a direct hit from a rocket and crashed into a dock with a bang. The other speed boat circled back behind the TITO IV to prevent any incoming fire from potentially hitting its props.

Captain John started calling out on the loudspeaker positions of the gangsters on the docks equipped with rockets. He wanted to try to ensure the ship would not sink under his watch.

"Behind the third armor car, port side, by the orange crate," the Captain cried out. All of a sudden majority of the gunfire shifted to Tito IV's control room.

Ron yelled out, "They're trying to blind us! Continue suppressive fire!" He then told David to get to the Captain. "Tell him to gun it as fast as he can. We're breaking through!"

David made it up to the control room, where the bulletproof glass was barely holding back the onslaught from the cartel. Captain John only had a small patch of the window not covered in cracks as he was steering the vessel. David told him to put the pedal to the medal and go maximum speed.

Captain John calmly replied, "Sir, this is a yacht. We do not have any pedals."

David sighed and said, "Flank speed, Captain."

The yacht then began to pick up speed quickly and darted past many of the armored vehicles. Several rockets were launched in an attempt to take out the helm of the ship but missed due to the TITO's ever-increasing speed and maneuvering. Ron quickly ran to the back with his LMG and began laying down suppressive fire so no more rockets would hit their weak backside and possibly immobilize them.

When they finally pushed past the harbor entrance and thought they had hit the open sea safely with everyone onboard, Captain John put the yacht in a steady idol about two miles out while everyone conducted a security check with Adam. At this time, Alex discovered Ron calling out on the floor at the back of the yacht. He had taken a bullet to his stomach and was bleeding profusely as he tried to put pressure on his wound. Adam summoned Jim to the main deck, where Ron was shaking and looked weak. It was at this time the remaining fast boat pulled up alongside the Tito IV.

Ron cried to Jim, telling him that he was in a tremendous amount of pain, and he needed medical attention right away. In a state a shock himself, Jim asked Captain John where the closest port of call was with adequate medical staff to attend to Ron's wound?

One of the only levelheaded persons onboard and the best to assess Ron's wound was Simon, due to his combat and medical history. Simon took a look at Ron's injury and agreed that he needed immediate medical attention or die. With the limited treatment that he could provide now, Ron had at most three to four hours before he would just lose too much blood and die. They quickly decided to take the fast boat to Costa Rica, where Ron could be hospitalized until he could recover enough to be immediately transferred to Jamaica.

Jim boarded the fast boat with Ron, and both headed full speed to Limon, Costa Rica. King, who just missed the conflict, rushed to the yacht's new location and boarded the Tito IV along with Simon and Adam and the Black Disciple Gang led by Leroy. King was enraged and wanted to exact a strike right this instant. They all concluded that there must be a retaliation attack immediately, but they need more intel. From what they gathered so far from various contacts, it seemed like El Capo was behind this attack. Leroy stated that one of his contacts on the police force just identified one of the bodies as one of Capo's top assassins, his right-hand man.

The El Capo Cartel cannot be allowed to attack the Marquis Cartel in Panama; that would show a sign of weakness. Leroy then received word about where the remaining cartel members were hiding. He summoned all of his lieutenants and ordered them to surround the six remaining armored vehicles that had transported the cartel to the port. They laid in wait for El Capo's Cartel to let their guards down as they celebrated and drank at an abandoned warehouse. When it appeared that most of their men were far from their armored vehicles, Leroy's gang slowly moved in and opened fire on the building, storming it and eliminating the majority of the cartel members.

Only one armored vehicle managed to leave the facility, while the other five were left behind. Two cars quickly sped after the solo armored vehicle, and a highspeed shoot out incurred. At the same time, Leroy's men took custody of the remaining cars, an added asset for the Black Disciples warehouse of artillery. Anyone found alive were gathered on their knees and bound. Those who could not stand on their knees were doused with gasoline and set on fire as the others watched. King stepped in and shot the first man in line seven times in the face without the slightest hesitation.

He roared, "Who sent you!" Leroy immediately translated so they would understand. No one said a word.

King smiled and said, "I already know who sent you." He took out an eight-inch bowie knife, grabbed one of the bounded men by the head, and slowly cut off his ear as he screamed in complete agony.

King threw his ear to the ground in front of the lot and said, "Ladies… I'm going to have a fun night with you." A chainsaw could be heard revving in the background. "We knew you were going to tell us nothing. I just wanted to do this for fun. You fucked with the wrong cartel, and it's time, as they say, to pay the piper. And a pound of flesh is what you owe. I love my job!"

The last armored car managed to give them the slip and disappeared in the night. Leroy told King, who erupted into a rage, beating one of the men to death with his fist alone.

When Jim arrived in Limon, he admitted Ron to the hospital for emergency treatment for his gunshot wound. During this time, Jim had to complete paperwork listing Ron's complete name, contact information, etc. When they asked for his insurance information, he told them the bill would be paid in cash. Due to this and the nature of the injury, red flags began popping up in the hospital reporting system.

As required, the hospital notified the authorities of the gunshot wound. Additionally, the two people involved stated that they were partners, and their address was an unknown island located outside of Miami. Payment for services rendered by the hospital was to be in cash, no insurance involved. They included Ron and Jim's last names in the report. When the Costa Rican Police Department received the hospital report, they ran the names through their police system as standard procedure. The results of each search revealed: report each individual to the FBI.

Noah, Captain of the Limon Police Department, called Special Agent Logan from the Miami FBI. He reported that Jim and Ron were both in the Limon hospital while Ron received medical attention for a gunshot wound. Jim was also there at this time, tending to Ron. Noah asked if Special Agent Logan had any special instructions. Logan instructed Noah to apprehend Jim on suspicion of money laundering, place a guard in Ron's room and wait for further instructions.

When the Costa Rican authorities arrived at the hospital to apprehend Jim, he was still talking about Ron with the doctors. He was obviously emotionally stressed, with one of the doctor's arms around his shoulders. As the police walked closer, the medical staff stopped them and told them that Jim's partner had just passed away and that it was not a good time to discuss any of the issues around the gunshot wound with him.

Little did the medical staff know that the gunshot wound was not the issue at hand, but Jim was to be arrested for another suspected crime, "money-laundering." The police continued to approach Jim, then handcuffed him and informed him of the FBI's instructions and that he was going to the Limon jail. When he got to jail, the first thing he did was place a call to King telling him of Ron's death, his arrest, and for him to take over the Cartel's operation in code.

At this time, the only remaining active partner of the Marquis Cartel was David, with King overseeing his safety. Their leisurely trip to Panama has been the ruination of not only a devoted love affair, an enduring friendship, and the biggest cartel the Caribbean Sea has ever seen. The El Capo Cartel had achieved what others had tried before, to destroy the most powerful cartel in the Caribbean. Once again, El Capo was in control and will continue to be for years to come.

Both David and King made sure that Ron's body was taken back to Miami and buried in the Martinez's mausoleum alongside Tito and the Martinez family. After which David took his share of the money that Ron had stashed in various bank accounts throughout the world and went into exile. King's criminal organization began scaling down the Marquis Cartel operations to blend it into their operations within the Caribbean Sea.

Jim, still distraught over the loss of his second love, became emotionally detached and depressed. He thought he was cursed to lose all those he ever loved and began pushing people away, deepening his depression. Jim had no fight left in him and constantly wished that he too died. He just wanted to be with the ones that he loved. A world without love was the worst imaginable torture to Jim, far greater than any prison sentence or punishment that could be handed down on him.

The Special Investigators began questioning Jim about all his affairs and his supposed connection to multiple drug kingpins and gangsters. They suspected him of being this mysterious "Big fish" they had been chasing all this time.

Jim just looked at them blankly with pain in his eyes, never muttering a word no matter how much they questioned him. Jim turned down several lawyers' requests that David tried to set up for him secretly. It seemed that Jim had just given up on life and would accept whatever verdict without a fight.

They extradited him to the United States, where he would have to stand trial on his pending charges. However, the government was still desperately trying to add new charges to Jim's initial indictment to make him out as the "King of the Caribbean."

On the fifth day of questioning, one of the detectives, tired of Jim's lifeless demeanor, tried to get an emotional response from Jim by blaming Ron's murder solely on Jim. He screamed at Jim, telling him that Ron would have never died if it was not for Jim's greed and his blatant disregard for the law and that he was a disgusting human being and deserved no mercy at all.

Jim may have felt all of this might be true, but as soon as the agent told Jim that, "Too bad for Ron that God doesn't allow fucking FAGGOT's into heaven," Jim lost it, headbutting the detective, breaking his nose and sending him crashing to the floor.

Jim went utterly psychotic. As spit flung from his mouth, he shouted that he was going to kill the detective and for him to mark his words as he leaped out his seat, trying to attack him. The detective wiped his nose with the cuff of his sleeve. He looked at the blood that dripped from his face, got up, and rushed at Jim, punching him repeatedly in the head.

"You've really fucked up now!" The detective then pulled out his gun, pressing it to Jim's head, and said, "I could kill you right here and now, and no one would be the wiser; no one will miss a drug lord faggot like you. Now you mark my words! I'll make sure your prison stay is absolute hell!" And then he slammed Jim's head against the table, causing Jim to blackout.

No one asked Jim any more questions, and his scheduled court date was fast-tracked. Before you knew it, the judge sentenced Jim to ten years in prison for money laundering and assault on a federal agent. Jim would spend his entire sentence at the high-security federal facility, "the United States Penitentiary Lewisburg," in Pennsylvania. The Special Detective stood idly by, snickering the whole time when the judge delivered the verdict.

To be continued…

In the next book

REVENGE: OF THE MARQUIS CARTEL

Jim's first agonizing year in prison will be the most dramatic period of his life. He has to endure the hell of being new meat in the grinder. During his remaining nine years in prison, he contacted some of the Mexican Mafia members and established more than a friendly relationship with them. Once he gets out if he gets out, will he or will he not rekindle his relationship with King and the Cartel that he's had so successfully built? The second love of his life, Ron, had been killed by El Chapo's organization. Revenge is on his mind. As we know, Jim's methods of operation paralleled King's as he used his versatile actions in bed as his secret weapon. Jim's soft side has virtually disappeared. Can anyone tap into it?

ABOUT THE AUTHOR
James Marquis

*J*ames was born the son of sharecroppers and grew up in tenement housing on a farm in Iroquois County, Illinois. At the age of thirteen, he and his family moved to a small village in the same county where he graduated high school. At the age of seventeen, he moved from the small village to Champaign, Illinois, the home of the University of Illinois, and he secured a position as a teller at one of the major banks. Because of his "Personality, Looks and Communication Skills," it was not long before he was promoted to head teller. During this time frame, he was drafted into the Army to supplement the surge of troops during the Vietnamese crisis.

His distinguished military career was recognized when he received a Bronze Star Medal. His training in the Army prepared him to pursue his life's dream of acquiring financial freedom. After he was discharged from the Army, he returned to the small Illinois bank and discovered it had limited promotional opportunities to achieve his dream.

James sought out and attained a position with one of the world's largest banks based in California, where he spent twenty-five years. During this time, he was recognized internationally as the bank's top motivational speaker. In the last ten years of his employment, he was Regional Vice President of Operations for northern California.

He was influenced to put his writing talents in book form by the author, Annie Prouix, who wrote the book "Brokeback Mountain." James is writing a fictional love trilogy that includes the books; "1968: A Vietnam War Love Story," which was influence by some events that took place before, during, and after his tour of duty in Vietnam, "the Marquis Cartel" a purely fictional tale and finishing off with "Revenge of the Marquis Cartel."

ABOUT THE BOOK

The Marquis Cartel is a continuation of "1968: A Vietnam War Love Story," the second book of a three-part Love series. Jim's first love, Tito, was killed in Vietnam. Tito's eternal wish was that he and Jim run his father's, Henry Martinez's, import/ export business located in Miami, Florida. Fifteen years after the war, Jim, with his new lover Ron, who he also served with in Vietnam, joined by their longtime assistant David, are now employed by Henry's import/export company in Miami. Henry gifted Jim a yacht that Jim named the Tito, which ended up serving as Jim's home office. Soon the small yacht started to feel cramped, and they needed to upgrade to the slightly larger Tito II.

But as their business grew, so did its employees. The business then acquired the "Tito III," a 130' yacht to replace the 90' Tito II. Now the Tito III crew had the proper accommodations to travel the high seas of the Caribbean to focus their efforts on the expansion of their import/export operation, thus allowing them to control all ports in the Caribbean Sea.

But something was not quite right, and the deeper they dug into the company's inner workings, so did the threat of danger. Jim, Ron, and David made every effort to ensure their personal safety and that of their crew. The Cartel had already been struck, but who ordered the hit and why? Do they stay in Miami, retreat to other ports of call, or just give up on everything?

www.ingramcontent.com/pod-product-compliance
Lightning Source LLC
Chambersburg PA
CBHW022037170626
46808CB00003B/1241